EYES OF WISDOM

THE WHITE BUFFALO WOMAN TRILOGY

EYES OF WISDOM

BOOK ONE

HEYOKA MERRIFIELD

ATRIA BOOKS
New York London Toronto Sydney

ATRIA BOOKS
1230 Avenue of the Americas
New York, NY 10020

BEYOND WORDS
PUBLISHING
20827 N.W. Cornell Road, Suite 500
Hillsboro, Oregon 97124-9808
503-531-8700 – 503-531-8773 fax
www.beyondword.com

Managing editor: Henry Covi
Proofreaders: Jessica Bryan and Meadowlark Communications, Inc.
Cover design: Carol Sibley
Composition: William H. Brunson Typography Services
Interior artwork: Heyoka Merrifield
Cover and epilogue artwork: Keith Powell

Library of Congress Cataloging-in-Publication Data

Merrifield, Heyoehkah, date.
    Eyes of wisdom : book one in The White Buffalo Woman trilogy / by
Heyoka Merrifield. — Beyond Words trade paperback ed.
        p. cm. — (White Buffalo Woman trilogy ; bk. 1)
    Originally published: Rainbird Publishers, © 1997.
    Includes bibliographical references and index.
    1. Indians of North America—Fiction. I. Title.
PS3563.E7445 E94   2006
813'.54—dc22
                                                                2006022895
ISBN-13: 978-1-58270-151-6
ISBN-10:   1-58270-151-2

First Atria Books/Beyond Words trade paperback edition November 2006
10 9 8 7 6 5 4 3 2 1

ATRIA B O O K S is a trademark of Simon & Schuster, Inc.

Beyond Words Publishing is a division of Simon & Schuster, Inc.

Manufactured in the United States of America

For more information about special discounts for bulk purchases,
please contact Simon & Schuster Special Sales at 1-800-456-6798 or
business@simonandschuster.com.

The corporate mission of Beyond Words Publishing, Inc.: *Inspire to Integrity*

Contents

Prologue

I dedicate this book to the memory of Auda, my mother. She joined the World of Spirit as I was writing *Eyes of Wisdom*. Mother was my first teacher, and through her I received the genic memory of our Cherokee ancestors. At the age of eighty-one she simply quit eating and after a short time peacefully crossed over. When I read the beginning chapters of this book to her, she seemed to enjoy them and I feel she would have liked the way it ended.

The myth of White Buffalo Woman is precious to me. It is the center of my ceremonial life. This book is a novel written from my imagination and draws from the many stories that I have encountered about White Buffalo Woman. I have also incorporated the other mythic themes and personal experiences that have come to me from the Great Mystery.

Many friends have helped and encouraged me as I worked on *Eyes of Wisdom*. I would especially like to thank the friends who assisted me: Patricia Smith, Liz Clow, Snow Deer, Sherm Williams, Tamara Kay, Pam Inverson, Keith Powell, Anders Abele, Tim Houck, and the staff at Beyond Words Publishing and Atria Books.

In celebration of All My Relations.

Chapter 1

The Twins of Night and Day

In the midwinter night, the glowing medicine lodge reflected its light on the surrounding snow. Inside, the Circle of Elders sat close to the warmth of the fire. The flicker of the council fire illuminated Night Eagle's hands as he signed the story of his history. The hand signals were like a mesmerizing dance. Owl, as most of his friends called him, wove the journey of his life with his weathered hands and his crackly old voice:

> *"In the winter of my birth, on the night that is the longest, my father, White Otter, was out hunting. It was a bad winter and there was much hunger in our village. The sky was clear and it was very cold*

1

in the Valley of the North Star. Otter had been tracking a deer for most of the afternoon and at last he saw his prey far ahead of him. He tried a shot, but misjudged his distance and the arrow went between the stag's front legs. Otter decided that he was too far away from camp to track the deer any farther and turned back toward the village..."

It was evening by the time he found the trail that led down the valley to his lodge and a warm fire within. The full Moon was rising and the night was as bright as twilight as Moonlight reflected from the snow-covered trees. The snow sparkled with all the colors of the rainbow as the glow cast Otter's shadow across the path.

Suddenly, White Otter saw the tracks of a buffalo calf crossing the trail in front of him, and he bent down to read the sign. One lone calf, no other buffalo tracks nearby. White Otter felt the spirit of the give-away and knew that the calf would give itself as food for his family. He offered tobacco to the powers of the hunt that had brought him this gift. He followed the tracks and saw that the lone young buffalo was having a hard time making its way through the deep snow. The snow had a strong crust that Otter could walk on top of easily as he neared the calf. He killed the buffalo with one arrow in its neck, then walked to the still body.

Dancing slowly around the calf, Otter sang an honoring song. The song spoke of thankfulness for the life of the buffalo that would bring life to Otter's family. It went on to say that one day Otter would die and give-away his body to the Earth. His body would feed the grass and the grass would feed the relations of the young buffalo within the circle of life. The buffalo had fallen next to the Medicine Tree where the People left their prayers and offerings.

Not far away in White Otter's lodge, his mate, Painted Fawn, was near her time of birthing. Grandmother Eyes of Wisdom was helping her to birth her first child. Fawn was worried about Otter being out so late; however, she was also hoping that his delay meant that his hunt had been successful and there would soon be meat in the lodge.

Grandmother helped Fawn into a squatting position as her contractions grew closer together. She fixed a backrest for Fawn to lean against and told her to try to relax between each contraction.

Otter was busy skinning the buffalo calf, so he was not aware of the approach of the mother buffalo. The cow had been searching for her lost calf and was tired from walking through the deep snow drifts. She was not in a good mood. She smelled her calf and felt the death in the air.

Startled by the dark shape between her and her calf, she charged.

Otter heard the crashing sound behind him and knew that his life was in danger. He turned and tried to jump out of the way of the charging buffalo. The snow crust gave way beneath his feet, and he was struggling to regain his balance when she struck him in his chest. The last thing Otter saw was the white Medicine Tree with the many tobacco ties and feather bundles tied to her branches. Each medicine object was holding a prayer gift to the tree. He thought, "What a wonderful place to die," as the tree grew brighter until he felt only the intense light.

Fawn cried out with relief as her son cleared the birthing channel and fell into Grandmother's hands. The full Moon was overhead and its light shone down through the smoke flaps. An owl called out through the clear, cold winter night. Fawn felt a radiant light in the lodge as she held her firstborn to her breast.

Eyes of Wisdom cut the umbilical cord with a flint knife and tied the end with sinew. She then embraced the mother and child and cried tears of joy. Fawn said that she was afraid that the calling of the owl had meant that someone had died.

When Fawn awoke with a sharp pain in her womb, twilight was showing through the smoke flaps. The contractions increased rapidly and as the Sun broke over the mountains, the second twin was birthed. As Grandmother put the second son into Fawn's arms, an eagle shrilled its call from far above the lodge. And so Grandmother named the twins Night Eagle and Sun Eagle.

Chapter 2

Grandmother

Owl was lying in the tall grass in the shade of the cottonwood trees. The spider he watched worked her spider magic and spun a beautiful web. He had been watching the colorful spider since she attached her first cord, and now there was a symmetrical pattern radiating out from the center. She then started spinning her web in a spiral, working toward the center.

This is how Grandmother Eyes of Wisdom found him, and she decided to lie down with him in the grass and watch the creation of the web. "What is troubling you, Little Owl? Your energy is heavy with sadness. What could be troubling you on such a wondrous spring day?"

The young boy continued watching each move the spider made as he replied, "Oh, Eagle and my cousins were just here and they wanted me to go hunting with them. I was watching the spider spin her trap and did not feel like hunting today. Sun Eagle called me 'Slow Owl' and said that I was lazy. My cousin Stalker said that I would rather be listening to old women's stories than to be out hunting and making meat for my family. Grandmother, what Stalker says is true. I would rather be here and learn about the spider medicine. Does that make me slow and lazy? Why am I so different from my twin brother?"

Grandmother's eyes twinkled as she spoke:

"Although you were born as twins, your brother and you have come into the world on different paths, like the many strands on that web. You and your brother will walk separate journeys in your life; on the other hand, you may notice how every strand meets in the center.

Your medicine power is the owl, and your brother's medicine is the eagle. Actually, the two animal powers are similar, for they are the two creatures that are closest to spirit. The eagle flies the highest of any creature and has the most powerful eyesight. In this way, the eagle can be seen as the creature closest to the heavens, and from that perspective, it is the power with the most expansive vision.

At night, the eagle is nearly blind, and it is the owl who has the most powerful eyesight. Both are messengers from the world of spirit; one of the light and one of the darkness. This is why the owl is called the night eagle like your namesake. Darkness is considered frightening, or even evil by some people, yet the darkness of the Sacred Void was the first power in all the universe. Out of this dark void all life was created, just as new life is created out of the darkness of a woman's womb.

My medicine is also the owl, and you and I see the world from a similar perspective. We want to see into the meaning of all that we observe and feel around us. You like to sit for half a day watching the spider because you are being taught by the greatest teacher of all, Mother Nature. Through meditative observance of the natural world, you will learn the language of Mother Earth and receive her wisdom."

The spider completed her spiral journey and now the shimmering web reflected the Sun as the gentle wind passed over it.

"The spider's home is a reflection of our life's journey. The cycles in nature turn in a circle like day and night and the movement of the seasons. In our personal journey, we travel in cycles on the Medicine Wheel of Life. We spiral in until we are in the center of the wheel where all is one. Your brother may seem to you like he is more powerful than you or has more fun because he is a good hunter. He may also seem more popular amongst the other young boys. Your power is a more quiet and subtle strength. It is the inner power of a medicine teacher and a healer. Like myself, your spirit came into this life to be of service to the tribe as a medicine person. The life of a medicine person may seem difficult at times, yet it is a rich and fulfilling life."

"It is time to start your medicine bundle, and you can start with this." Eyes of Wisdom removed her crescent Moon pendant and placed it around Owl's neck. "This mother-of-pearl Moon was given to me by my teacher. She traveled toward the setting Sun for several Moons until she arrived at the Great Waters. In these waters are little creatures that live inside small lodges similar to a turtle's home. This crescent Moon is made from one of these lodges and holds the power of the Great Water, of the night light, and of the female powers of cycles." Owl's body tingled with the medicine power emanating from Grandmother's Moon shield.

• • •

On another bright spring day, when the birds were singing their medicine songs, the twins walked along the creek looking for a good fishing hole. Inside a leather pouch hanging from Eagle's shoulder were freshly dug Earthworms, a few hooks carved from bone, and two cords made from braided plant fiber.

They found Eyes of Wisdom sitting by the stream with her medicine bundle spread out beside her. She held an owl wing in her hand and was letting the water of the stream wash over it. Excited by the marvelous objects in her bundle, the brothers crowded close and sat down with her. Sun Eagle asked why she was putting her doctoring fan into the creek. "I am clearing the unnecessary energy from my medicine feathers. When I am using the fan for healing, you have seen me pat the sick person's body and brush the energy field around their body. The fan cleanses the body's aura and some of that sickness might stick to my fan. Sometimes, I shake it out to the winds or burn sweetgrass smoke to cleanse it. Other times, I pat a tree or a plant and ask it to take the negative energy. And sometimes, I let the creek purify my feathers and healing stones, as I am doing now."

Owl asked about a very long and narrow feather that was bright blue with red underneath. He had never seen a bird with such a feather. Grandmother said:

"Once I traveled far to the south, to a desert land where people live on high, flat mountains. Their houses are made of wood and mud. They are built close together, so the whole village looks like one lodge.

I went there to learn from a medicine teacher. While I was at the Flat-Topped Hill Village, a holy man from a land much farther south visited the tribe I was living with. He had many long feathers of all the colors of the rainbow, which he was trading to the People. The People of the Lying Down Mountain use these feathers in their ceremonies to decorate their masked dancers.

I made friends with this medicine person and learned very much from him. It was he who taught me the name of the star clusters that I teach to you on our night walks. It was also he who taught me how to measure the seasons with the place on the horizon from which the Sun rises using the pointer stones.

Remember the spring celebration ceremony we had recently at my Medicine Wheel of stones? As we stood on the hilltop and watched the Sun rise over the tall pointer stone, that place marked the time of equal day and equal night. Also, the same stone marks the direction of true east.

As summer progresses and the Sunrise walks north along the horizon, the days get longer than the nights, until the longest day of the year comes. Another pointer stone marks the place of Sunrise at the time of midsummer. The days then get shorter as the Sunrise walks south along the horizon, until they are equal again at autumn time. The Spring and Autumn Equinoxes share the same Sunrise marker. The Sunrise continues to move south until at midwinter it is the shortest day of the year—the day you were both born.

This and many more wondrous teachings came from the People of the Rainbow Feathers. They live in a land that has no winter or snow. It is green and warm all year long and it rains much of the time. The teacher told stories of fantastic creatures, and the feather you hold is from a colorful bird in this faraway land."

Sun Eagle thought about the Earthworms and wondered if they would catch a big fish that day. Night Eagle thought about going to the Medicine Wheel, often at the time of Sunrise. He wanted to look again at the pointer stones and measure the coming of summer, autumn, winter, and next spring.

• • •

Later that spring, the twins were helping Grandmother gather the herbs she used in healing. They were picking flowers and tying them in bundles. "This blue flower is for placing on cuts and wounds," said Eyes of Wisdom. "We put three pinches in hot water and place the tea and wet flowers on the cut; this will keep the wound from getting infected." Grandmother was looking intensely at the flowers and picking one here and one there. First, she had given tobacco to the flower beings for their help in healing.

She asked the boys if they could see anything different in the flowers she chose. "Look at the energy that surrounds each flower. Gaze in the area just above the flower and relax your eyes and let them go out of focus. There will be a light surrounding the flower that looks like the waves of heat rising from a rock that is in the direct Sun." Owl followed Grandmother's instructions and could see an increased light around the flowers that she picked. Eagle could see only flowers, so Grandmother had him touch each flower to see if he could feel the difference in the ones she was picking. "The ones with the brightest light have more life force and make a stronger healing medicine. People also have an aura that extends out from their bodies. The light surrounding people can tell a healer much concerning an illness or how a person is feeling. Practice looking at the auras of people at different times and see if you can find out what colors an angry person's aura has. Look at different people when they are experiencing different emotions and then we can discuss what each color and each shape means. Medicine healers can read much from the light body of a person after they learn the skill of seeing energy."

Night Eagle allowed his eyes to relax as he watched Grandmother. He did not see colors, only a bright light surrounding her body.

Chapter 3

Shining Woman

When it was time for the twins to experience their rites of passage, they walked together to the mountain. It was in the Sunset direction from North Star Valley where the tribe lived. It was very hot as they climbed and soon their bodies glistened with sweat. As they neared the top, it became windy and cold, like they had walked into another season, and they had to wrap themselves in their buffalo robes. Although they climbed the mountain together, they chose places a distance apart for their vision quests. Alone, they spent four days and nights fasting, not taking food or water. In this time of passage from boyhood to manhood, they prayed for a vision that would help to guide them in their life journeys.

Sun Eagle looked over the valley in which he had lived his life. He thought about the things that brought joy to his life and how he could best serve the community of his tribe. He loved to hunt and was better at the bow then any of the other boys. He knew he was going to be a hunter and perhaps a warrior.

Sitting all day on a large flat rock was not comfortable for Sun Eagle; also he was hot and thirsty. By the afternoon of the fourth day he was very weak and exhausted. He fell asleep, and during his medicine dream the cry of an eagle overhead awoke him. Sun Eagle offered tobacco to his medicine power animal and to the Spirits that had brought him the dream.

On Owl's second night on the mountain, he was sleeping on his back, wrapped tightly in his buffalo robe. He was drawn into wakefulness by a powerful dream, and as he moved a rattlesnake sang near by. Fear surged through his body and he wanted to see where it was, yet the robe was bound so tightly against the cold that he could hardly move. As he struggled to free himself from his wraps, the rattlesnake rattled her alarm again.

By now Owl was very awake and he realized the snake was coiled up on his chest. Also, he realized that this was a powerful visitation by a medicine animal. He thought of how the movements of snakes are slow and fluid. Micking these movements, Owl slowly rolled over until he felt the weight of the snake leave his chest as she slithered away.

Night Eagle did not sleep for the rest of the night and he thought of how the primary medicine power of a snake is healing. As he lay marveling at the stars, he remembered the teachings that Grandmother Eyes of Wisdom had given to him. She had shown him how to gather and dry the healing herbs and how to use them. She had taught him with her wisdom and experience. Most of all, she had taught him with the way she lived her life. Every morning and evening she would offer tobacco and say her prayers to the Sacred Powers.

Owl knew more than anything that he wanted to be a healer and medicine teacher like Eyes of Wisdom. He would be a shaman healer and live a life of service to the tribe. The medicine dream that had awakened him felt like it was saying something important about his life as a shaman.

Later, while walking down the mountain together, the twins described for each other their medicine dreams. The two boys had always been connected in many ways, and it was not a surprise that their visions contained similar symbols.

In his dream, Sun Eagle was alone hunting a buffalo with only a spear. He ran up to the big bull and threw his spear into its heart. The bull fell down dead and Sun Eagle approached cautiously to skin the buffalo. As he moved closer a white snowy owl appeared, sitting on the buffalo. Sun Eagle felt frightened at the sight of an owl, the bird of death, looking into his eyes as he was awakened by the call of the eagle.

Night Eagle saw a white buffalo in his dream, and it led him to the tribe's sacred Medicine Tree. This ancient tree was the oldest grandparent to the other surrounding trees. It was to this powerful entity that the People brought their prayers and offerings.

In Owl's vision, the white buffalo walked into the tree. Night Eagle followed the radiant buffalo until he was touching the Sacred Tree. A flood of emotion surged through his body and the tree became the entire universe. The tree's branches were the different families: one branch being the birds, another the animals, another the people, and so on. On the branches, the leaves were the different types of each family of beings. In touching the tree, Owl could feel all the life of the universe and how everything was connected to the one trunk. The feeling reminded him of the prayer that is said as people enter the Sweat Lodge: "All My Relations." Owl felt that the meaning of his dream would unfold as he meditated upon it.

After considering it for a short time, Sun Eagle decided to follow his vision dream. He would hunt alone with only a spear and kill a buffalo. Owl told Grandmother Eyes of Wisdom what Sun Eagle was planning to do. She replied, "When a young, dependent boy becomes an independent man, a type of death occurs. It is the death of dependency and the birth of independence. Many young men have to act out in the outer world that which is happening in their inner world. This is why young men have to risk death in doing wild and dangerous tasks." She suggested that Owl accompany Eagle on his hunt and that they should seek out the help of Longtail.

Chills ran up Owl's back as he said to grandmother, "Do you mean the one the People call 'Crazy Claw?' People say he is crazy and that he eats small children. Some people think he is an evil spirit. No one ever goes near Death Canyon where he lives because it is haunted."

"His real name is Longtail, the mountain lion, and that is also his medicine. He is an old friend of mine and if you say that Grandmother Eyes of Wisdom sent you, he will help. He is very wise in the ways of animals, and going to him may save your brother's life."

With their hearts pounding, the twins entered the Canyon of Death. Their stomachs felt like dark holes and their mouths were too dry to swallow. There were animal and human bones dangling from the trees. The skulls of animals were looking out at the trail from many directions.

As they walked farther into the valley they came to an eerie Prayer Tree. It had many tobacco ties and bundles hanging from the branches. The strangest thing of all was that the tree had a beautiful woman's face in the middle of the trunk. Owl was too enthralled with the beauty of the face to be afraid, and he reached out to touch it. He saw that the face had been carved into the living trunk of the tree. As he ran his hands over the carving, there was a crashing sound. Owl was jerked upside-down and found himself dangling from a tree with a rope slipknot around his ankle.

Sun Eagle laughed hysterically as Owl swung from the snare trap tied to the top of the tree. When his laughing subsided, Eagle went over to help his brother get out of the trap. As he reached out to help Owl there was another crashing sound, and now both brothers were hanging from ropes that were tied around their ankles.

Suddenly, a monster jumped out from behind the Sacred Tree and started dancing around the twins. It had large, bulging eyes and long, pointed teeth. The shapeless body was covered with ragged hair. It laughed madly and said, "What meat hangs in my traps today? Hah! Nice, juicy boys!"

After swallowing his heart back to its rightful place in his chest, Owl could see that the monster was a man. His face was hidden behind a hideous, carved wooden mask and his body was covered by strips of cedar bark. This must be Crazy Claw, from whom they had come to seek help.

"What brings you boys into Death Canyon, the haunted land of Crazy Claw?"

Owl answered that Eyes of Wisdom had sent the brothers to ask Longtail for help. Crazy Claw removed his mask and bark robe, revealing a slight-bodied man with intense, kind eyes.

"My brother Sun Eagle had a dream on his vision quest that told him to kill a buffalo, alone, with only his spear. Grandmother said that you are wise in the ways of animals and could help my brother."

Longtail pulled them down and the three walked into his camp. The camp was wondrous. There were animals who were as tame as the village dogs. A deer came up and nuzzled their hands, while rabbits scampered around the boys' feet. The lodge skins were painted with animals that looked so alive that Owl expected them to jump off the covering. There were more of the amazing carvings and everywhere there were ingenious traps.

Sun Eagle asked, "Why do the animals not run away from us?"

Longtail said that he had trapped them as babies before their eyes were open, so he had become their father. A mountain lion walked out from his lodge and rolled over on her back so Longtail could scratch her neck.

Owl came up and stroked the huge cat's fur and she purred while draping her tail over the boy's arm. "Why do the paintings and carvings feel like they have the inner life of a living creature?" asked Owl.

"Most people paint pictures of things they see to represent the animals, birds, or people," replied Longtail. "There is another way to approach painting. Our Father is the Great Spirit and our Mother is the Earth; together they create all life. If a painter can enter into the Sacred Void, the womb of the Creatress, and create from that place, then the paintings will awaken with an inner life. It is our birthright to create life through our own creations because we have inherited that power from our Parents. If we create from our own heart centers and from the Sacred Center of the Universe, then our creations may wake up with a life force of their own. The World of Spirits chooses to come into the World of Substance when we create art from this Center of Creation."

Longtail brought out the longest spear the twins had ever seen. Sun Eagle could hardly pick it up. "I cannot throw this spear. It is much too heavy for me," said Eagle.

Longtail said he would accompany the brothers and explain how to use the large spear.

They went to where there were many buffalo tracks leading to a place for drinking water. Here Longtail had Eagle dig a hole into which he could fit his body. He then had Eagle dig a small hole and plant the spear in the ground at an angle so its flint point was a few feet above the ground. Brush and leaves were scattered over the spear to hide it from view.

When a buffalo cow and calf came down for a drink, Eagle would jump up between the cow and calf. The buffalo would charge at Eagle, and at the last moment Sun Eagle would jump into the hole and the buffalo would impale herself on the spear.

As a buffalo cow and her calf walked toward the watering hole, Eagle lay silent in the hole. When the calf was near him, he jumped up waving his arms. The calf bolted in fright and his mother charged at the creature that was endangering her calf. Owl saw only a huge cloud of dust when the cow reached Eagle, and he approached with apprehension when the dust settled.

Longtail's plan had worked perfectly, although the dead buffalo had landed above the hole and Sun Eagle was trapped under her body. Owl and Longtail were relieved when they could hear his muffled cries. The Sun had moved a hand's width across the sky before they could dig the boy out from beneath the buffalo. "Whew!" said Sun Eagle. "Until now, I never realized how really bad a buffalo smells."

Eagle thanked Longtail for his help in fulfilling the vision. Longtail shrugged his shoulders and said, "I have enjoyed watching because I thought that I would never find anyone foolish enough to use this great spear."

Owl asked why Longtail did not return to the People's village. His art would bring joy and beauty to the tribe and his traps would help the People to hunt. Longtail said that his creations frightened the tribal members and that he was too different from the other villagers. "They think I am crazy and do not want me in the village."

He said he could live alone because his creations are his children and the animals are his friends. He then asked the twins not to tell the tribe what his camp was like. If the People were not afraid to come to the Canyon of Death, then the hunters would come and kill his tame animals because his pets would walk right up to them.

As the twins started off for the village to get help in bringing home the meat, Longtail left in a different direction for his valley. The brothers had not gone far when they came to a large herd of buffalo that stretched in both directions as far as they could see. As they tried to decide which direction to walk around them, there appeared a bright light in the middle of the herd. The glowing shape dazzled their eyes as it moved toward them. Both of the brothers thought of their medicine dream.

It was not a white owl or a white buffalo. It was a beautiful woman dressed in a white deerskin dress. Her dress was decorated with porcupine quills of all the colors of the rainbow. Eagle plumes were tied in her long, black hair and to the fringe on her dress. She carried in her hands a bag decorated with the symbol of the Morning Star in quillwork. Owl had never seen an aura that was so bright and that extended so far. He could feel its touch from a great distance, and it reminded him of the feeling in his vision when he touched the Sacred Tree.

Sun Eagle was stricken by the incredible beauty of this woman. His body still tingled with the heat of the recent kill. He knew that he had to possess this shining woman and he told Owl that he would take Shining Woman for his wife.

27

Owl said, "Truly this is a medicine being walking partly in the World of Spirit and partly in the World of Substance."

"Then sit, Slow Owl, and pray," spat Sun Eagle as he ran toward Shining Woman. As he drew near to her, the light surrounding her increased until Owl felt like he was looking at the Sun, and he was temporarily blinded. When the light dimmed and he could see her again, she was standing alone, and lying there at her feet were weathered human bones. As Owl approached Shining Woman he took out his tobacco pouch and offered it to her. "I can see that you are a Goddess from the World of Spirit. What message do you bring to my people? Is it death, as has come to Sun Eagle?"

She said:

"Be at peace; I bring your people healing and life. Your brother and I were married and lived our life together. Time had no hold on Sun Eagle and me as we passed into a World within the World where we now walk. In this other World, fifty winters have passed for your brother, although for you it was but a short time. As was his desire, Sun Eagle and I shared a life of plenty and happiness: hunting, gathering, and making love medicine together. After a long and full life he died of old age.

Now go to your village and say that a medicine priestess has come to give them a gift that will bring them peace. Have them tie two lodges together to create a Medicine Lodge and I will come. Do this in the time of the painted trees when the day and night are equal. Gather all the People, including your friend Longtail, to the Council Circle."

Chapter 4

The Sacred Pipe

Surrounded by the painted autumn-colored trees, the Medicine Lodge stood in the middle of the village. On the Equinox, as the Sun rose, Shining Woman walked out of the east. Gathering all the tribe into the large lodge, she then placed eight people in a circle in the center. Longtail was in the east, Eyes of Wisdom in the west, Shining Woman sat in the south, and Sky Bear was in the north. To the southeast sat Night Eagle, Snowdeer was in the southwest, Grandmother Redtail sat in the northwest, and Rainbow Hawk was positioned in the northeast. In the center of the circle there was a small fire that illuminated the faces of the council members.

Shining Woman said that when she left the Council Circle, Moonflower should take her place in the south. She said that the eight-sided Council Wheel should meet often to discuss the problems, ceremonies, and visions of the tribe. She took a large pipe in two parts out of her bag and set it in front of her. She said that the council should always start by smoking this pipe. The pipestone was red like the blood of the People, and it was a gift from the Earth. She then lifted the bowl to the stem and said, "In celebration of All My Relations," and joined the two together.

"This pipe is to be your altar and a way to gather all the Powers of the Universe. When you breathe out the smoke, it will take your prayers to All That Is. The pipe bowl is in the shape of the feminine powers, and the stem is of the masculine powers. As the two are joined, there is a perfect balance—the balance we will all become as we join these two powers in our inner self. The tobacco is a gift from the Plant People who sacrifice themselves in the creative fire, that we may all live. The World of Plants also brings its healing energy to our ceremony. When we place the tobacco into the pipe, we honor each power, starting with

32

the Mother Earth and the Great Spirit. Then we invite the Grandparents of the east to come to the altar, the Helpers from the south, the Ones who come from the west, and the Spirits from the north. There is tobacco for the Sacred Tree that is in the center of our wheel when we Sundance, and for the Rainbow Powers that surround us with their protection. When the World of Plants is called to our ceremony, the plants bring all their gifts: herbs, food, fiber, and learning from our ancient teachers, the Trees. We honor all the Medicine Animals, each with its own special power that they bring to our circle. We invite our Ancestors, the Spirits, and the Teachers of all the Worlds who have something to teach us or have something to help us with in our venerable ceremony.

Before we light the fire to the tobacco and smoke, we again honor the Powers of the six directions by offering the pipe to them first: the Sky, the Earth, and the Grandparents of the four directions. As we smoke the Sacred Pipe, we offer into it our prayers for healing, peace, and for understanding of our place on the Wheel of Life. With this smoke, we send our voice to the

Universe, and this smoke takes our prayers to our Helpers in the Sky and in the Earth.

After we have entered the Sacred Circle with the pipe, we can speak only the truth as we sit in this eight-sided Council Wheel. When it is necessary to pass a law for the benefit of the tribe, we will speak only over the pipe as it is passed around the circle. The pipe will be passed Sun-wise around the circle until everyone agrees on the new law. The one law that all laws must be measured against is: 'How will the new law affect the children for seven generations?' This law is represented by the small fire that is in the center of our circle."

Shining Woman then gave the Sacred Pipe to Eyes of Wisdom and said that Grandmother would be the new keeper of the pipe and bring it to council whenever they met. "In time, people may want to make personal Ceremonial Pipes to help them and to be an altar in their own lodges. The pipe will bring peace and healing to all who use her in a sacred way." Shining Woman asked Moonflower to take her place and sit in the south of the Council Wheel. "I would like for the council to talk about ending Longtail's banishment. When we speak over the pipe within the Council Circle, we will always start in the east." She took the Council Pipe from Eyes of Wisdom and gave it to Longtail.

Longtail smoked for a while in silent meditation and then spoke over the pipe:

"For years I have lived alone, and it was a time of vision quest and of joining with the Creative Center of the Universe. Now, as I sit with Shining Woman's Pipe in this Council Circle, I feel it is time to bring the gifts that I have been given into our tribe. I will tell you of the story of my brother so the Council Wheel may better understand what happened. There was no intent in my heart to harm my brother the day he was injured. I wished only to play a trick on him, like the many he had played on me throughout all my life. My older brother Red Bull was always making life difficult by teasing me, tripping me, or embarrassing me.

At that time I was studying the habits and the medicine of a family of badgers. I wanted to learn their way of life and I wanted to build a trap that could catch one of them. One day my trap finally worked and I had a live badger in a small cage when the door snapped shut. I was running back to camp when I saw my brother Red Bull coming up the trail. I ducked behind a tree and was going to jump out and scare him, when I had a better idea.

I ran back and hid the trapped badger near her home. Then I tied the largest crystal in my collection with a string that went to the door of the trap. Scattering a few smaller crystals on the trail leading to the large one, I hid in the bushes. Bull picked up one of the crystals and then saw the large one. I held my breath as he squatted right in front of the caged badger and reached for the large crystal. As he picked it up the door flew open and the badger sprang out and bit into his bottom. Bull screamed and jumped straight up into the air—at least as high as my shoulder. He would have flown higher but he hit a branch, flipped in the air, and came down on his arm.

This ferocious little animal was only protecting her home and was not to blame for the accident. She was following her nature and instinct. The growling badger, still holding on to him, shook his bottom a few more times before she walked off feeling like the chief of all badgers.

I heard his arm snap when Bull fell and knew that he was injured. It seemed as if I were standing within a bad dream. I wished that I could undo what had happened to Red Bull. His arm healed poorly and he was not able to follow his dream of being a hunter and warrior. I felt guilty and estranged from the tribe. Many of the People thought I should be banished, and I agreed."

The pipe was then passed to Night Eagle, who spoke next. "This injury was an accident and was not planned by Longtail. He has suffered the punishment of many lonely years of banishment, and now I think that it is time to make peace with him and let him return."

The pipe was passed Sun-wise to Moonflower, who spoke next. "Longtail's trick caused a painful injury. What about the loss of a hunter to Red Bull's family? I think the banishment is just and Longtail should not be allowed to return to the tribe."

Snowdeer received the pipe into her hands and then spoke. "I think what is needed is healing medicine songs to heal the wounds to Red Bull's family, for with the banishment they have lost the help of both of their sons. I say, let there be a healing ceremony first and then let Longtail return to us."

Grandmother Eyes of Wisdom spoke next over the pipe. "We must ask permission from the mother of Red Bull and Longtail before the banishment is ended. It is she who has also suffered, with one son losing the use of his arm and one son taken from her by banishment. Also, let us look to see how Longtail's coming back will affect the children for seven generations as Shining Woman has instructed us to do."

Grandmother Redtail held the pipe as she talked from the northwest of the council. "The gifts of new ways of painting, carving, and catching animals will be of benefit to the children for many generations. If we accept Longtail back into the tribe there should be a law accompanying these new traps. That law should say that traps will never be used on humans; traps will only be used on animals that are needed for our food, our clothing, or our lodges."

Sky Bear took the pipe from Redtail and spoke his thoughts. "These traps will make the gathering of our meat much easier. It will mean less work for our hunters, and men who are too young or too old for hunting can set these traps and will be able to help in the making of meat for our tribe. I feel Longtail should return and teach us the use of the kinds of traps for different animals."

Rainbow Hawk said, "I agree with letting Longtail return to the tribe. I will be responsible in seeing that no one uses the traps against humans. If we agree upon this new law, it will be my duty to see that the people keep the law."

Longtail received the pipe and spoke. "I will live with what the council decides. I will return only if each person in the Council Wheel feels it is right to end the banishment."

When Night Eagle was handed the pipe, he said, "I have spoken," and he handed it to Moonflower.

Moonflower now spoke. "I see the wisdom of all that was said in this wheel and agree. Longtail may return, but his traps may never be used to harm any of the People."

The Council Circle realized they had reached an agreement and all together they said, "Ho!"

Shining Woman said, "See how the Council Wheel has turned and has brought a new law to the tribe. It is a balanced way of finding the correct action to take concerning a new way for the People. When the council meets again you may follow the same pattern when talking over the Sacred Pipe." She then took the pipe, and raising it to the sky she said, "In celebration of All the People," and separated the pipe from the stem. Shining Woman then placed the bowl and stem into the Morning

Star bag and handed it to Eyes of Wisdom. "When the time is right to pass the pipe to another keeper, you will know who it is. That person must care for the pipe and bring it out for the appropriate ceremonies."

She said to all the people gathered together in the ceremonial lodge, "I now bid you farewell. Use the pipe in a sacred manner and the surrounding tribes will see reflected in the life of your village the peace and prosperity it will bring. If they ask to be given the teachings of the Sacred Pipe, and the council agrees, you may give it to them so this wisdom may grow throughout All the People."

Shining Woman then walked out of the lodge in the direction of the prairie. Owl felt a great loss at her leaving and began to follow her at a distance. As she came out onto the prairie, there was a herd of buffalo that stretched out to the horizon. Without looking back, she walked straight toward the herd and started shining brightly like the first time Owl had seen her when she suddenly appeared before him and his brother Sun Eagle. The light increased until it became dazzling white and then it faded away. Where Shining Woman had walked he saw a white buffalo walking toward the herd. Owl offered tobacco to the Earth and to the Sky for the medicine gift that White Buffalo Woman had given to him and all the People. After the white buffalo joined the rest of the herd, Owl turned away and started walking back to his village.

Chapter 5

The Courting of Moonflower

Owl was walking through the meadow in late autumn in the time of morning frosts. He saw someone digging in the Earth and decided to see who it was.

He found Moonflower digging camas roots in preparation for the Chinook Dance that would happen in mid-winter. She was covered with perspiration as she plunged her digging stick into the ground.

Without hesitation Owl asked if she would like him to help her. As he started digging, Owl realized that it had been many cycles of seasons since he had talked to Moonflower away from the activities of the village.

43

Owl had always felt strongly attracted to Moonflower, yet in his shyness, every time he tried to talk to her his voice would not work. The last time he had attempted to tell her how he felt was when he found Moonflower and two companions picking flowers.

He had determined that he would approach the three young women and ask her to join him in walking back to the camp. Owl imagined holding hands with Moonflower as they walked through the woods, with him expressing to her his strong feelings.

He walked up to her and said, "Like you would with walk to em." The backward, upside-down words cracked through the silence.

Moonflower smiled at him. He felt the butterflies fluttering in his stomach increase their activity. There was a heat below Owl's belly that rose quickly up his body to his face.

Moonflower said, "Night Eagle, are you blushing?"

Gray Dove said, "Perhaps we should call him Red Owl."

Prairie Rose chimed in, "He looks like a bull elk on the scent of a female during mating season. Perhaps we should call him 'Horny Owl.'" The three women broke out in laughter.

The heat that Owl was feeling turned into a raging fire, and when he looked down his body was bright red. He turned and ran so fast it felt like he was flying over the ground, until he reached the stream. Jumping into the creek, Owl let the water flow over him while his heart pounded in his ears. He had never felt so close to death, yet he had never felt so alive.

The memory of this encounter made Owl's stomach feel uneasy. As he dug up the roots, Owl tried to build up the courage to speak his feelings to Moonflower. Suddenly Stalker was standing above them holding a huge wild turkey in his hand. He threw down the great bird and said, "Moon-flower, I have brought you this turkey so you may have meat in your family's lodge. Owl, when did you start doing woman's work? Will you start wearing skirts next?"

Owl felt the heat rising in his body again and remembered the times that Stalker had beat him at wrestling. He knew if he attacked Stalker, he would be even more shamed with Stalker sitting on him. Owl turned his back on him, smiled at Moon-flower, and walked away.

Owl found Grandmother smoking White Buf-falo Woman's Pipe at her Medicine Wheel. When the ceremony was finished, he spoke. "Grand-mother, I need the help of your wisdom. I have a strong feeling of love for Moonflower, but it is dif-ficult for me to speak to her." Owl then described the misadventures he had experienced over the years when trying to talk to Moonflower.

Eyes of Wisdom gazed into the distance as she spoke. "With love and relationship, there will always be confusion and pain. When my mate Singing Elk died, I felt so much pain that I have never spoken about it until now." Owl noticed there were tears running down the wrinkles in Grandmother's cheeks like little streams through canyons.

Owl felt sad as Eyes of Wisdom continued:

"Also the most wonderful joy I have ever experienced is the time that Singing Elk and I shared together. So, if I had not opened myself to my greatest pain, I would not have received my greatest joy.

The power of wisdom helps little when we approach the great mystery of love and relationship. Using our mind to find the trail that leads to the understanding of this mystery will not help when that trail comes to the river of romantic love. The water is swift and deep. If we try to stay on this trail of understanding we will only be helplessly swept up by the current of the river.

If we sit on the bank and contemplate the river of love and life, we will never experience our full humanity. When one feels the way you do about Moonflower, it is best to jump into the churning water. Only then will you experience the exhilaration of the fast current, the cleansing of your spirit, the peril of death, and the water of life.

You spoke to Moonflower with your actions when you helped her to dig camas roots. She knows that to help her, you put yourself at the risk of being teased by your friends. Stalker demonstrated his affection for her with a showing off of his powers as a hunter. You showed your affection for Moonflower with an act that came from your heart. You are on the right path. Continue to speak to her with acts of kindness from your heart and she will hear you with her heart."

Three seasons after speaking to Grandmother, Owl was walking through a grassland and noticed that the flowers of summer had gone to seed. He remembered sitting on a mountain during this time of summer and that there were still spring-like flowers on the high slopes. Breathing heavily as he labored up the mountain, Owl approached the place where snow still lingered near the top. Here the delicate mountain flowers were still in bloom. He realized that if he picked the flowers to bring to

Moonflower, they would be dry and dead after the long journey back home.

The only thing that Owl had with him was his breech cloth, which he removed and soaked in a spring. He then prayed to the spirits of the flowers and asked them to give-away so he could show his love for Moonflower. Carefully choosing each flower as Grandmother had taught him, he placed them in his wet breech cloth. Walking down the mountain naked, he soaked the cloth often to keep the flowers fresh.

As he neared the village, he saw Moonflower in the same meadow where he had found her digging camas roots before. Walking toward her, Owl suddenly remembered he was naked. Quickly he removed the flowers and replaced his cold, dripping breech cloth. As he approached her with the flowers in his hand, Moonflower returned Owl's shy smile.

Moonflower received the flowers in her hand and was enthralled by their beauty; she had never seen some of the mountain blooms before. Owl tried to speak but found that his tongue was tied in a knot.

Signing with his hands, he spoke with sign what his voice could not say:

My heart is to your heart
as the Sun is to the Moon

the eyes of the Sky that smile upon the Earth
What I feel is too expansive to say with words
so I express my feeling for you
in kindness and signs
It would bring me joy
to share my life with you
and together with love
we will travel down the river of life

The Sun reflected on Moonflower's long black hair and also on the tears on her cheeks. Owl reached out to touch the tears and then touched his chest over where his heart was beating. His breast was wet and he realized that he too was crying and now their tears were joined.

Moonflower embraced Owl and the couple shared love medicine together in the meadow under the Sun and surrounded by the give-away flowers. The following spring, the meadow was covered with more blue camas flowers then anyone could ever remember seeing in one area. So the place was given the name "Camas Flower Meadow."

Chapter 6

The Give-away

After the coming of the Sacred Pipe, there were many years of peace in the Valley of the North Star. Then some of the hunters started to be attacked in the north when they were out on the prairie. In the time of the long nights, the Council Wheel met to discuss and reach an agreement concerning the neighboring tribes. Since the tribes to the northeast were making war on the People of North Star Valley, it was decided that they would not hunt or travel unnecessarily in that direction.

Owl suggested that they could invite the People of the Prairie to join the pow-wow during the salmon run next year. "If we were to spear fish and feast together they might not feel like making war with us. After singing, dancing, and gambling at the stick game, we would be like brothers."

Moonflower spoke of how severe the winters are on the open prairie. Without the high mountains to obstruct them, the winds howled down from the north, bringing with them extreme cold. "I think the harsh climate makes the Prairie People tough and fierce. If we send someone to invite them to a pow-wow, they may attack the one who tries to speak for us."

Grandmother Eyes of Wisdom said, "White Buffalo Woman's Pipe has brought peace amongst the people of our village. Our councils have been more orderly, and the decisions we make are more in balance.

I would like to see the teachings of White Buffalo Woman and the Sacred Pipe given to our neighbors. The Prairie People will probably not make war on our messengers if the ones we send are healers and peace chiefs. I feel all the neighboring tribes would benefit from the sacred gift.

Longtail, you are the most skilled at making ceremonial objects, and you know how to wake them up with the life force of all the powers. This winter you can carve eight pipes for the tribes that are our neighbors in the eight directions."

When he held the pipe, Longtail answered, "It would be an honor for me to make Council Pipes for our neighbors. Into each pipe I will call the powers of the four elements, the planetary powers, and also the powers of the Sun and Moon. We can talk about which tribes will receive the pipes and I can conjure the specific totem animal of each tribe into their pipe."

Soon the pipe returned to Eyes of Wisdom. She said that Moonflower, her mate Night Eagle, Longtail, and she would be the ones to give-away the Sacred Pipes to the neighboring tribes. "The Prairie People will not feel threatened if four medicine people, one of them being a grandmother, come into their camp. We will leave in the spring, travel all summer, and return in the late fall."

The council then decided which tribes would receive the eight pipes. The four medicine chiefs were to go east first to the People of the Sky Stones. After gifting the Blue Stone People, the four would walk Sun-wise around the North Star Valley giving away the pipes. After they gifted the Prairie People in the northeast with the last pipe they would return home to the Village.

At the last pow-wow, Longtail had traded for red pipestone from the lands far to the east. He had recognized the stone instantly as the one White Buffalo Woman's Pipe was made from. All winter, Longtail worked on carving the pipes and on the ceremonies to wake them up. The women of the tribe decorated the pipe stems with quill work. Also, they made fringed deerskin bags decorated with the Morning Star Planet to hold the pipe. As the snows of winter thawed and the river swelled, the eight give-away pipes were completed.

Soon the first flowers began to appear, and with the coming of the robins, the tribe knew that winter was over. The Earth was now totally awakened with the new life of spring, and the Council Wheel met to discuss the journey to the surrounding neighbors. Longtail brought the eight pipes that the tribe had worked upon through the long winter. He placed one pipe bag in front of each one of the eight council members.

Eyes of Wisdom said that after the council had smoked the Pipe of White Buffalo Woman, they would do the Sacred Pipe ceremony with the new pipes. As they smoked the give-away pipes, each council member would gather the energy of all the council meetings of all the winters since White Buffalo Woman had given them this ceremony. The beauty of the ceremony and the power of the Council Wheel that had been given to them would be passed on to their neighbors. The council members sat in silent meditation smoking the new pipes and charging them with the peace and prosperity that White Buffalo Woman's gifts had given to their tribe.

Eyes of Wisdom, Moonflower, Longtail, and Night Eagle traveled with only light backpacks. They planned to live on the abundance of nature and the gifts of the tribes they visited. They would have to travel at a good pace to circumvent the entire Valley of the North Star before winter came. As they camped each night, Longtail would set snare traps and there was meat to eat almost every day. The abundant roots, seeds, berries, and greens completed the diet of the travelers.

A few days into their journey, the four were camped in a meadow with an expansive view of a mountain range. The Sun was setting behind the mountains, painting the sky with many colors. Moonflower and Owl sat in an embrace watching the Painted Cloud Beings.

Owl noticed Eyes of Wisdom and Longtail sitting together a distance away. They were also viewing the Sunset in silence. Owl had never seen Grandmother's aura so radiant. The more he looked, the more he noticed that Longtail's light body also had a new glow about it. In fact, the auras of his two old friends seemed to merge together, forming one light. The twin light body looked like the feeling Owl experienced when Moonflower and he shared love medicine together.

Rising early the next morning, Owl went down and bathed in the nearby stream. On his way back to the camp, he checked the snare trap and found a rabbit giving-away for the campers' breakfast. Carrying the rabbit, he returned to camp and was surprised to see Eyes of Wisdom and Longtail sharing one blanket. A sense of joy filled Owl as he looked down upon his medicine friends entwined in each others' arms. Although Grandmother had been a young woman when Longtail was born, the two seemed a perfect match for each other.

The meadow was all aglow that morning, as they left a little later than was usual. The spring vegetation had enjoyed sharing the love medicine with the two couples, and the light bodies of the flowers were much brighter than when the campers had arrived.

The Moon had decreased from full to crescent and was starting to grow again when the travelers started seeing the signs of the tribe they were seeking. A few days later they saw the village in a valley below the hill where they were standing.

The People of the Blue Stones were excited about the arrival of guests and had made plans for a great feast. A large elk was brought in by the hunters and had been roasting all day. The bounty of spring accompanied the feast.

While feasting, they told the stories of the many winters since the two peoples had met at a pow-wow. After the feast, Eyes of Wisdom asked that the Council of Elders come into the center of the celebration next to the fire.

She then took out the pipe bag and asked Owl to tell the story of the coming of White Buffalo Woman and her Medicine Pipe. After Owl's story, she told the story of the Council Wheel and how it had helped the tribe throughout the past years.

Grandmother then removed the pipe from the Morning Star bag and said, "In celebration of All My Relations," as she joined the bowl and stem. The People's eyes went wide when they saw the beautiful red pipe. A blue stone was inlaid into its stem, surrounded by colorful quill work. She then did the ceremony of White Buffalo Woman and passed the pipe to the elders to smoke. She asked an elder who was the healer-priest of the tribe to become the keeper of this Council Pipe.

The chief elder thanked Grandmother for the gift and said they would incorporate it into their ceremonies. The chief said that in their tradition, women never sat in their council meetings. He was not sure about using that part of the Council Wheel that White Buffalo Woman had taught.

Grandmother said the Blue Stone People were a balanced people, which showed that their traditions were good.

"Perhaps it is time to see if the traditions might grow into a more powerful balancing way by using White Buffalo Woman's Council. When the woman's way of seeing the world is brought into your council, it will bring a new power into your wheel. This medicine priestess has brought a new way to our people, and you may try it and see if the wheel turns in a beauty way for your people.

We are calling for a pow-wow in the Valley of the North Star. It will be four winters from now, at midsummer, and there will be a Sundance. At that time, a council member from each of the eight tribes that has received a Ceremonial Pipe will meet in one council. We can speak at that time about how this new council wheel has affected all the different tribes. In that way, we can learn from each others' experiences and bring more power into White Buffalo Woman's Ceremony."

The medicine friends traveled for five Moons before they had given seven of the Sacred Pipes to the tribal peoples who surrounded the Valley of the North Star. The last pipe was to be given to the warring People of the Prairie. The Prairie People moved camp often, following the great herds of buffalo wherever they went. After weeks of wandering on the prairie, the travelers found the tribe's trail. As they neared the village, a war party ran out and surrounded them. The party was made up mostly of young men painted for war and creating more noise than danger.

Eyes of Wisdom spoke. "We have been traveling all spring and summer to bring a wondrous gift to your people. Go now and tell your chief that four medicine people are bringing a gift from White Buffalo Woman."

As the travelers neared the village, Owl noticed there was refuse piled up around the unpainted lodges. The camp seemed disorderly and unkempt in general. There was no talk of a welcome feast and no one seemed happy to see the guests.

The villagers crowded around them and one large man stepped up and said he was the chief of the tribe. Grandmother asked the chief to call his council of elders together so she could present them with a gift. The chief, who was called "War Cloud," said that he had no such council and that he made all the decisions for his tribe. He said he had four lieutenants, six sergeants, and the rest of the men were dog soldiers. The chief sat down and had his lieutenants sit down behind him.

Owl spoke, telling again the story of how he and his brother found White Buffalo Woman and of the Sacred Pipe she had brought. Grandmother told of the Council Wheel and how it had helped to keep order within the village for the past several winters. When Grandmother took out the give-away pipe, the people gasped. There was a buffalo carved behind the bow in the red pipestone. The stem was decorated like the pipe bag, with many colored porcupine quills in the design of the Morning Star. It was obviously the most beautiful thing made by human hands they had ever seen.

Eyes of Wisdom gave the Prairie People the pipe ceremony as White Buffalo Woman had taught her. She then passed the pipe to the chief and his lieutenants to be smoked. The ceremony was ended as she raised the pipe to the sky and said, "In celebration of All the People." She separated the bowl from the stem, placed them in the fringed bag, and then handed it to War Cloud.

It was obvious that the chief knew he was holding a precious treasure in his hands. He said the pipe would become the center of his ceremonies. War Cloud then said that he did not see the need for a Council Wheel.

Grandmother told him that if it did not work, he could disband it. If it worked as well as it had in their village, it would give the chief time for more important things. If the everyday problems and ceremonies of the camp were handled by the council, then War Cloud would have more time for hunting and preparing for war parties. She then invited him to come to the Sundance pow-wow. "It will be good to talk then about how White Buffalo Woman's Ceremony and the council have benefited you and your people."

Chapter 7

The Full Circle of Tribes

F our winters had passed since the travelers had given the eight Council Pipes to all of the neighboring tribes. White Buffalo Woman's ceremony was now being used by the eight Peoples. The coming together of the tribes was to be the largest pow-wow gathering in anyone's memory. The great event was to be called "White Buffalo Woman's Sundance" by the medicine people, who had been planning the ceremony for many seasons.

There were numerous ceremonies in the winter and spring, building energy and excitement for the midsummer pow-wow. As the various tribes began to arrive, they were assigned to camp in areas that had been prepared for them. Soon there was a great nation of tribes camped along the North Star River and the larger creeks that joined the river flowing toward the star that does not move.

On the morning of the longest day of summer, the elders of the eight tribes gathered in the center of the camp. There was a small fire where the Sacred Tree would stand and Grandmother Eyes of Wisdom sprinkled cedar leaves on the fire and offered prayers to the forthcoming ceremony. As dawn approached, the elders blessed themselves with the fragrant smoke as it danced swirling toward the sky.

The glow on the horizon became brighter and as the Sun slowly rose the elders stretched their hands toward the it. They celebrated the Sun's gift of life with deep appreciation and then placed their hands over their hearts, accepting the blessings from Father Sun.

After the Sacred Tree was placed in a hole where the fire had been, every aspect of the building of the lodge became a medicine symbol, meant to collect healing energy for the Sundance ceremony. The Sacred Tree was a cottonwood chosen for her beauty and symmetry. She was a forked tree to honor how all aspects born into the world come in as sacred twins. Day, Night, Woman, Man, Past, Future, and all other physical powers reflect the double nature of the created world. As spirits become part of Mother Earth, they dance a two-wayed path. The Sundance Tree was also a reflection of us, as we draw nourishment from the earth like the tree's roots. We too reach toward the sky and draw nourishment from the Sun and the air.

The Sundance Lodge was built to accommodate more than a hundred dancers. In honor of White Buffalo Woman, the Sundancers arrived wearing their beautifully painted skirts. The skirts were girded with wide belts covered with colorful quill work.

Grandmother Eyes of Wisdom was the Sundance chief and was in charge of the ceremony. She looked like a Goddess, with her rainbow-colored Sundance vestments and her long white hair flowing around her. Longtail had trapped an eagle and she was tethered to the branches of the Sacred Tree. Tied to the trunk of the Sundance Tree was the head of the buffalo that had given-away its life for the great feast that was to follow the four days of fasting without food or water.

Grandmother sang the morning song as the Sun rose and shined his light into the door of the lodge. The singing of birds on the crisp, damp, morning air joined Eyes of Wisdom's song. Then the Sundancers piped their eagle bone whistles to the Sunrise.

Next, the steady heartbeat of the drummers started, and the singers sang throughout the day and late into the night. As the music played, the Sundancers danced back and forth to the tree until there were little paths trodden into the grass radiating out from the center. With each dance they gave a prayer to the Sacred Tree of Life that stands in the middle of the Universe.

The third day, when the people who needed healing entered the lodge, was the hottest and most difficult for Sundancers. The people to be healed removed their moccasins, so, like the dancers, they were barefoot upon the sacred ground of the lodge. When fasting became the most painful, it was also the time that the most energy was expected from the dancers to help Grandmother. While the dancers gave their support to the healing ceremony, Eyes of Wisdom doctored the sick people with her owl fan and her otter hide.

The last part of the ceremony was the bringing of water into the lodge for the dancers to have their first drink since the beginning of the four-day ceremony. After four days of fasting, the water seemed like the most precious substance in all the World. This sacredness was etched into the Sundancers' beings and would be remembered whenever they drank water again. When all the dancers had drunk the blessed water, the tethered eagle was released, connecting the prayers of the Sundance to the Heavens, as the Sacred Tree had connected the prayers of the Sundance to the Earth.

The feast was a festive celebration and gave the neighboring tribes the opportunity to socialize, trade, and play games. The young people searched the other tribes for prospective mates and friends. The boys competed in an arrow-throwing game in which the first arrow is the mark and the one whose arrow lands the nearest to the first is the winner. The men of the tribe bet on their sons or clan members and many finely decorated shirts changed hands.

After the feast, a council was held with one member of the eight neighboring tribes sitting next to a council member of the North Star Valley. When White Buffalo Woman's Pipe was passed around the council there were sixteen speakers.

As the eight tribes told of their experiences of the past four winters, there was an agreement that the Sacred Pipe and the Council Wheel were wondrous gifts. Each tribe had stories to share about how peace and prosperity had grown because of White Buffalo Woman's Ceremonies.

The Blue Stone People spoke concerning how having women sit in their Council Wheel had brought much wisdom and understanding into the problems and ceremonies of the tribe. There were many skills that the women had to offer. In the past, they had never been given the opportunity to contribute these gifts. The Council Ceremony had caused more harmony within the tribe and also within individual families.

The Sacred Pipe had been a wondrous tool to gather the Powers into a ceremonial circle. Many of the Blue Stone People now had individual Ceremonial Pipes that they used in personal ceremonies. It helped the People to center their energy and enter into a quiet, meditative inner place. White Buffalo Woman's Pipe Ceremony was being used by the healers, priestesses, and priests, and as an altar for personal prayers.

The People of the Prairie told of how having a Council Circle had changed the life of their village. The war chief now sat in the south of the Council Wheel and took an equal place in governing the tribe. The other council members brought their expertise to the wheel, and conditions within the tribe had improved greatly.

With a more orderly village the camp did not have to move so often. This gave the People time to be more creative. The lodges now had medicine paintings on them and the hunters were better equipped with finer hunting tools. The warriors had more time to plan and prepare for war parties. The Prairie People then challenged the other tribes to a contest of bow shooting and also a game of lacrosse to include all the tribes.

As Grandmother sat in the Council Wheel she realized that her work in this life was finished. The many visions she had dreamed concerning how the people could live in peace were now set in motion. She also started to see more deeply into the wisdom hidden within White Buffalo Woman's Council Wheel.

Chapter 8

The Council Wheel

The green of summer gave way to the yellow, orange, and red of autumn. Winds shook the bundles of herbs and roots that hung drying on racks next to the tribe's lodges. A council was called together by Grandmother Eyes of Wisdom. She said, "In two Moons, in the time of winter, I will pass White Buffalo Woman's Pipe to a new keeper."

Longtail spoke over the pipe. "Many winters have passed since White Buffalo Woman first formed this Council Wheel and gave us the teachings of the Sacred Pipe, and now Eyes of Wisdom says it is time to pass the pipe to a new keeper. This cycle has indeed been a time of peace and prosperity for our village, as White Buffalo Woman said it would. I trust our Grandmother in the west to know when the time is right for changing."

When Owl took the pipe he said, "The medicine of White Buffalo Woman is still working in our wheel and the passing of the pipe from Grandmother will also bring peace and abundance."

When Moonflower took the pipe she said, "Who has the experience and understanding of our Grandmother and can fill her moccasins? Perhaps we should wait for someone to reach her level of power before a new pipe keeper is chosen. It might bring bad luck to pass it on too early."

Snowdeer had her turn to speak over the Sacred Pipe. "It is Grandmother Eyes of Wisdom's place to decide when to pass the pipe on. When this happens we should have a ceremony, sing songs for the passing of the pipe, and celebrate the future. It should be an honoring ceremony for Eyes of Wisdom and the new keeper."

Eyes of Wisdom spoke next over the pipe:

"I have been honored by sitting in the west of our Council Wheel. Over the years I have marveled at the wisdom of how the wheel turns when we take our turn speaking Sun-wise around the wheel. For me the wheel has come alive and has a life of its own. We have all held an equal part in the balancing way of this Council Wheel and how it works.

Soon it will be time for me to choose someone to take my place in the west. First I will tell you what White Buffalo Woman's wheel has taught me. I see that she chose all of us for the special power that we personally brought into one of the eight directions of the Council Wheel. To the east, White Buffalo Woman chose Longtail, who knows how to speak from the man's perspective, the artist's path, the creativity way, and the contrary, who is the heyoka. When it is time to replace Longtail, someone should be set in the east who can view our laws from that type of perspective. Longtail's replacement would need to be able to turn a new law upside down so we can see how ridiculous this law could be; it should be a person who can make us laugh. The new council member in the east should be a sacred clown so we will not get too serious.

The southeast should have a peace chief who can speak from that power. Owl has always spoken from the perspective of what will bring peace, and this should continue.

In the south, we need to have a war chief, someone who will confront the new law and make war upon it. Through this combative vision we will see a different aspect of the law. Making war is always one possibility, although it shows wisdom when the peace chief speaks first.

There should always be someone to speak for healing and we should have a medicine singer like Snowdeer always sitting in the southwest. This direction of the Council Wheel should see how to bring healing to the new law.

In my direction in the west we need to have someone who can see the new law from a woman's Creatress perspective, and understand how the law will nurture and affect the children for seven generations."

The glow of the central fire reflected on the faces of the council members as they nodded in agreement. Grandmother knew that White Buffalo Woman's Wheel was coming alive for the seven elders as it had for her. Eyes of Wisdom continued to weave the web connecting the individual gifts that each member had given to the whole circle:

"When the pipe is passed to the northwest, it should be to someone who can see the effects the law will have on all of the members of the tribe. This place needs to have a chief who is a leader and can govern the People within the new law.

We need to have a person like Sky Bear, who is wise in hunting and the way of the workers, to sit in the north. That person can always see how the new law will affect those disciplines and can speak for all of the hunters of the tribe.

In the northeast is Rainbow Hawk, who is skilled in knowing how to encourage the People in the keeping of the new law if it is agreed upon by the Council Wheel. Hawk has always shown skill in keeping the laws of the tribe.

This is the wisdom that White Buffalo Woman's Council Wheel has taught me over the past winters. If we use the wheel as White Buffalo Woman has taught us throughout the last cycle, then it will always turn in a beautiful way. It will help us live a life of balance within the tribe."

Chapter 9

Crossing Over

In the last Moon of autumn Longtail noticed that Eyes Of Wisdom had been very distant and seemed to be pulling away from him. One cold, crisp morning, as the frost began to cover the painted leaves, he approached the subject of what she was feeling.

"Little Moon Bird, I have noticed that you do not seem to be present much of the time when we are together. Have I done something that has offended you, or is your body not feeling well?" Longtail asked with concern.

Grandmother looked into Longtail's eyes with such love that he knew all was well between them. She embraced him and said, "There is something I must tell you and I would like to speak of it in ceremony. Prepare a Sweat Lodge for us. In that sacred space I will be able to give-away to you the burden that is in my heart."

Grandmother's small dome-shaped Healing Lodge was by the creek, whose little waterfalls were beginning to form ice crystals. The lodge was about chest high and could seat about four people comfortably. It was made of red willow saplings, pushed into the ground, bent over, and tied together. The willow structure was then covered with buffalo hides. Longtail had a good campfire burning and was heating many fist-sized stones as Grandmother approached. "Have you prepared the Sweat Lodge for our ceremony, Little Kitten?" asked Eyes of Wisdom.

"All is ready after we offer tobacco to the creek and ask her to help us in the lodge, as I fill the gourd with water," replied Longtail.

They both crawled into the lodge and closed the flap while saying, "All My Relations." In the darkness of the Sweat Lodge it felt like they were sitting in the womb of Mother Earth. In a hole by the door the rocks were glowing red with the energy of the fire. The glow left the rocks as Grandmother poured water on them and they hissed forth steam. The blackness was complete now and when Grandmother spoke, it was like a voice coming out of the Sacred Void.

"When Singing Elk died I thought that I would spend the remainder of my life without a mate. When you came into my life as my partner it was a great blessing that has brought me much joy. Little Kitten, you have been a supportive, thoughtful, and kind friend. I celebrate all the time together that the powers have gifted to us.

I feel the cycles of life are now calling me into the Spirit World, and I am complete with the journey I have taken as Eyes Of Wisdom. My only regret is leaving you behind, and I am having difficulty speaking of our separation."

Longtail felt the sweat dripping off his face onto the Earth and knew it was mixed with tears as he spoke. "Little Moon Bird, I knew when we were joined that you had lived many more winters than I and would probably join the World of Spirit before I did. Being with you has been the greatest joy of my life and I shall treasure every winter that we have shared. Although being separated for a time from you will be the greatest pain of my life, I trust your wisdom in the time of this passage. I would not want you to stay any longer than you feel is right, only for my sake."

The wind had kicked up during the ceremony and it froze their braids into solid ice on their way to the lodge. Sitting by the fire they gave each other back rubs as their hair thawed out.

That winter, Grandmother Eyes of Wisdom called the Council Circle together for the passing on of the Sacred Pipe. Longtail spoke first as always. "Grandmother's life has always been an example of how to walk the medicine path. She has been for me an image of how to be in my later years as my hair turns white. Also, she has taught me how to open my heart to the wonders of love and companionship. Everything in nature has its season of life, death, and rebirth. Never will there be someone whom I will miss more than Eyes of Wisdom when she crosses over."

Night Eagle took White Buffalo Woman's Pipe and said, "I feel so much pain that there is no room for words. I feel like I am as empty inside as the night sky would be if there were no Moon or Stars. I can't imagine a world without Grandmother, whom I love above all the People." He then sang the Sundance medicine song that Eyes of Wisdom had taught to him.

Moonflower said, "Grandmother has taught me how to be a person of power, how power is an inner quality that does not have to be spoken about. It is felt surrounding Grandmother with whatever she is doing."

Snowdeer sang an honoring song to Grandmother:

Grandmother, you have nurtured us like a
mother bird with a nest of hatchlings
You have always given your teachings and
your gentle healing to all the People
Eyes of the night seeing into the mystery
of creation, the womb of the Sacred Void
You have seen into the deepest mysteries,
learning to touch the Sky
while touching the Earth
Like the owl who sees clearly at night,
Grandmother has been our Eyes of Wisdom

Grandmother took the Council Pipe and spoke. "For eighty winters I have lived among you and now the World of Spirit is calling me to the other side. As winter brings to a close each cycle of seasons, so death brings to a close the cycle of our lives. I have loved all of you as my children and you must remember, after winter comes spring; also, after death come birth and a new beginning."

Grandmother Redtail said, "We have been children together and have grown old together. We have been companions and friends all of our lives. I know not where I end and where you begin, and I feel like a part of myself is leaving."

Sky Bear spoke, saying, "Always it was you, Grandmother, that I could come to. Whenever there was a question that troubled my heart, you were there for me. You have been my greatest comfort in life."

Rainbow Hawk spoke. "Grandmother, it was your wisdom that opened the teachings to me. The Council Wheel that White Buffalo Woman gave to us has always worked so beautifully; even so, it was you who brought the Council Circle teachings to life for me. Your understanding saw into the inner workings of the wheel, and you have shown all of us its inner relationships."

After the pipe had completed the circle and was again in Grandmother's hands, she stood and walked over to Owl. "Owl has been my apprentice all of his life. He has always shown a natural wisdom in the ways of the Earth and her creations. He has become a healer and a man of peace. To him I now give White Buffalo Woman's Sacred Pipe. He will be the keeper until he chooses to pass the pipe on to another medicine person."

Eyes of Wisdom then took Painted Fawn to her place in the west and asked that the council consider Fawn to be the new medicine person sitting in that part of the wheel. "She is a wise woman and knows the mysteries of healing herbs."

Grandmother then lit a braid of sweetgrass from the small council fire in the center of the circle and purified the wheel with smoke. Last, she blessed herself with the smoke. She then walked out into the frigid winter night without her buffalo robe. Grandmother Eyes of Wisdom was never seen again.

Chapter 10

Vision Quest

The next spring Owl was very troubled. The tribal members were coming to him with more and more questions. He did not feel that he had grown enough white hair to be the primary medicine teacher for the People. The pipe was now in his keeping and it seemed too powerful a responsibility. He decided to go on a vision quest and pray for understanding of the things that were troubling him.

Wearing the mother-of-pearl Moon pendant that Grandmother had given him and carrying White Buffalo Woman's Pipe, he walked toward the mountains. Choosing the highest mountain, called "Mother of the People," he started his climb.

He struggled all day through the dense forest; in the afternoon the trees started to thin and Owl knew he was getting toward the top. The trees appeared to be ancient, though they were only as high as his knees. The appearance of the trees gave Owl the feeling that he had become a giant towering over the forest.

Night Owl had heard stories all of his life about the little people of the mountains. He stopped in front of a small, ancient tree at the top of a hill and took out his tobacco pouch. As he sprinkled tobacco over the little tree he prayed, "Little People who live within the Earth, accept this tobacco as a gift while I walk through your village. You are welcome to come to my vision quest circle as I sit on the mountain for the next few days."

Soon Owl was at the summit of Mother of the People Mountain and he felt like he was at the top of Turtle Island. There were many small piles of stones that had been used as altars during other vision quests throughout a great expanse of time. He could see North Star Valley below him; to the west, south, and north were mountains that spread out to the horizon. He chose a spot where he could see in all directions.

To the east he could see the stream beside which the tribe's lodges were set up. To the south Owl could see the Sunset Mountains that overlooked the lands of the People of the Blue Stones. To the west he could see the country he had traveled to with Eyes of Wisdom so many years ago. To the north past a distant range of mountains lay the lands of the Prairie People.

He started gathering rocks together and placed eight large stones in the eight sacred directions of the Medicine Wheel. At the center he stacked the remaining rocks into an altar onto which he placed the Morning Star bag containing White Buffalo Woman's Pipe. He had started his fasting that morning and was very tired from the climb. He took the Sacred Pipe out and smoked as the Sun set over the mountains in the west.

He sat naked on his buffalo robe in the cold night and watched the stars in the Jaguar Constellation as it danced around the star of the north that does not move. The hair on the back of his neck tingled as he heard a mountain lion scream ten steps behind him. Owl's instinct was to jump up and run, although he knew he could not outrun the longtail. Also, if the Great Mystery were taking him in death as he sat in prayer, then he would accept his fate. The mountain lion screamed many more times in the darkness, and with the coming of dawn Night Eagle turned to see the longtail. A huge owl was sitting behind him and flew over his head in the direction of the rising Sun. Owl felt that he had died that night and his medicine power had given him a rebirth with the coming of a new day.

With the appearance of his medicine animal, he knew that the powers of the Universe were coming to his ceremony. Owl thought much about his life and about the loss of his father, his brother, and now Grandmother Eyes of Wisdom. Death and the loss of his loved ones seemed a harsh way for the Universe to arrange his time here. (This is perhaps why people have named the "All That Is" the "Great Mystery," and that mystery may be what has sent me on this journey to find "My-Story.") Perhaps Grandmother had been right when she said that she felt the spirit of Owl's father, Otter, had come into Night Eagle as he was being born. She thought that Otter's love for Fawn was so great that he could not stay long in the World of Spirit, and had returned to be with her through Owl.

For four nights Owl sat in his Medicine Wheel praying for a vision to bring peace to his heart. Owl had fallen asleep on his last night on the mountain and he was awakened by a strange noise. He heard the percussive sound that the male grouse makes, and it seemed to be coming from within his head. He was having a medicine dream when the drumming came and he sat thinking about the meaning of the dream in the glow of twilight. As the Sun was halfway above the horizon, two bucks walked in front of the rising disk.

Night Eagle felt that the powers had been dancing with him in his vision quest. First the longtail that was an owl, then there were strange Rainbow People in his medicine dream, and now the coming of the two deer on his final morning. He knew that with time the symbols of the visiting animal powers, and of the People of Many Colors in his dream, would reveal their mysterious meaning to him. Owl thanked the Spirits for coming to the ceremony and then walked back down the mountain to break his fast.

Chapter 11

Owl's Sundance Vision

Owl's long hair had grown completely white since his vision on Mother of the People Mountain. There was another great pow-wow gathering being planned in the Valley of the North Star. The central ceremony would be a Sundance celebrating the coming of White Buffalo Woman and the teachings of the pipe. White Buffalo Woman's teachings had brought peace and prosperity to numerous tribes as her Ceremony of the Pipe had spread. The dance was to be an honoring of this wondrous gift that White Buffalo Woman had given to all the People.

Owl was given the honor to be the Sundance chief. On the first morning of the ceremony the spot where the Sundance Tree would stand was marked with a stake. Then the Sunrise direction was marked to help position the door so the first rays of the Sun would shine into the lodge. Owl was smudging with cedar smoke and placing another stake in the ground east of the Sundance Tree toward the Sun. As a small group of medicine people turned away from the east and the Sunlit sky they looked toward the west and saw it was as black as night. Arched over where the Sacred Tree was to be placed, against the black sky, was the brightest rainbow that anyone had ever seen. It was a big medicine sign and Owl expected something powerful to happen.

The work of setting up the Sundance Lodge took most of the day. The Sundancers prayed with the Sacred Pipe to the forked cottonwood tree that would be used in the lodge. After thanking the Sundance Tree for her sacrifice, they cut her down and carried her to the center of where the lodge was to be built. The Sacred Tree was set into a deep hole and stood with her branches and leaves shimmering in the breeze. Around her, twelve forked posts with the limbs removed were placed in a large circle twelve paces from the center. Long, thin lodgepole pines were placed through the fork in the tree and tied to the twelve posts. The lodge now looked like a Medicine Wheel, with roof beams forming twelve spokes leading to the Medicine Tree. Around the circumference of the lodge were placed young fir trees that provided privacy and shade for the dancers. An opening in the fir trees was left in the east to be a door for the Sundancers and the Sunrise.

When the construction of the lodge was complete, the black sky of the west struck the ceremony in a tremendous storm. There were several old weathered Sundance Trees from past dances standing in the meadow near the lodge. It was the custom to leave the center tree standing and let it fall down from natural causes. One of the old trees was the tree from Eyes of Wisdom's dance honoring White Buffalo Woman many winters past. Lighting struck Grandmother's tree, knocking it to the Earth, and Owl sensed that Eyes of Wisdom had joined the ceremony. The whole camp was torn apart by the strong winds and almost all of the tribe's lodges were broken. Miraculously, the ferocity of the storm did not damage the Sundance Lodge.

The Sun was setting in the west as the dancers entered the lodge; the black sky was now hovering over the east. Marking the place of Sunrise in the east was a rainbow pillar shooting straight up from the horizon. As he danced to and away from the tree, Owl thought of his vision quest dream where he had seen the People of the Different Rainbow

Colors. He thought of how the lodge had seemed to be protected from the fierce storm by the rainbow. His medicine dream took on new meaning and he started to see what the symbols were saying. While he danced in the Sacred Sundance Lodge the language of the symbols started to open up to Owl.

Grandmother Eyes of Wisdom had once taught him that the trees and plants communicate with each other by using unseen and unheard energy. When a tree is cut down, all her relations experience her death. That is why she always had Owl honor and thank a tree or plant before he cut it down, or before he picked an herb. When he prayed to a tree all her relations also felt his prayers.

Grandmother had said that when anyone was sick or tired they could stand next to a tree, hold the trunk, and ask the tree to take their pain. She taught Owl to feel the energy the tree pulls from the Earth with its roots and then share with the tree and let that power flow into his body.

As Owl danced he realized that all the trees were receiving the prayers that the Sundancers gave to the Sundance Tree; not only the trees in North Star Valley, but perhaps all the trees on Turtle Island or even all of the trees on the Earth.

Night Eagle could feel the teachings Grandmother had given to him about how a tree breathes. She had said, "A tree breathes in once every day and out once every night. We humans, who breathe many times a day, are so fast when we walk by a tree that the tree sees us as we would perceive a lightning being. When we dance in one place for four days in the Sundance Lodge the tree can see us for the space of four of her breaths. In this way we can have a closer relationship with the Sacred Tree."

Grandmother also said, "The air we breathe in, which gives us our life, is the air that the tree breathes out. Also, the air we breathe out is the air the tree needs for her life. In this way the People receive the breath of life that the trees give-away to them."

All the teachings that Grandmother gave to Owl were becoming more clear as he danced in and out of the Spirit World. The vision of the Tree of Life from his first vision quest was now the tree that he danced to. He danced for all the trees, all the birds, all the animals, and all the People. Remembering his vision of the Rainbow Warriors, Owl danced to all the tribes of all the other islands across the Great Waters until he was dancing to All That Is.

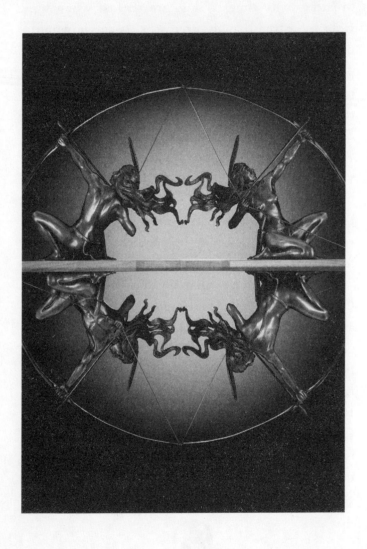

Chapter 12

Rainbow Warriors

That fall Owl called together the council for a meeting. When it was his turn to speak over White Buffalo Woman's pipe he told the circle about his vision quest:

"After the passing over into the Spirit World of Grandmother Eyes of Wisdom, I was very troubled. Seeking understanding, I went on a vision quest. After a time of fasting on the mountain, I had a medicine dream that I will now tell. There were many people coming to Turtle Island from across the Great Waters. Their appearance and clothes were very strange and unlike any that I had ever seen, even at our pow-wows of many tribes. These people were of different colors and they soon started making war on our tribes. They even made war on each other because of their difference.

The wars caused famine and disease and the spirit of our people almost disappeared. White Buffalo Woman's Pipe Ceremony was remembered by a few of the original tribes of Turtle Island, so the spark of life still remained amongst us. The ceremony of White Buffalo Woman helped to keep us connected to our roots even though our way of life here was completely changed.

Then there arose certain ones from the New Peoples who turned away from making war on each other and from making war on the trees, animals, and the Earth herself. These New People who embraced peace could see the balance that was in our Mother Earth. They recognized that all the People were one. Although we were raised in separate tribes and had diverse customs, they could see through the differences and embraced all the People as their relations.

I have not told the story of my medicine dream before because until now its meaning was unclear to me. But the dream became clear as I danced in the Sundance Lodge last summer. At the end of the dream all the People of the Many Colors and all the tribes of Turtle Island walked off together toward the east holding hands. In the place of the Sunrise was a newborn white buffalo calf.

• • •

During the Sundance I felt like the rainbow was protecting our ceremonial lodge from the storm that had destroyed all of our pow-wow camp. While dancing I saw that the People of Many Colors, who embraced the unity of all tribes, were the People of the Rainbow. The Rainbow Warrioresses and Warriors embraced peace and saw that we are all related. The Rainbow People were not called warrioresses and warriors because they were waging war on other tribes; rather, they were making war on the parts of themselves and their culture that were out of balance. In discovering an inner balance, they found harmony with all life. The spirit of the original People of Turtle Island and White Buffalo Woman's Pipe Ceremony helped to bring about this change.

I saw that each person has a birth, child-hood, and maturity. The declining years, death, and then rebirth follow. Each age of the World also has its cycles, and we are going to experience our time of declining with the coming of the Rainbow Tribes.

With the end of our way of life there will also come the birth of a new way of life. When the New Peoples connect with the Spirit of the Earth and the ceremony of the original tribes from Turtle Island, and the Spirit of the Earth and the cere-mony of the islands they came from, they will see the new vision.

From White Buffalo Woman, Grandmother Eyes of Wisdom, and our other teachers, we have been given a precious, sacred gift. The wisdom of our elders helps to guide us on our personal path and teaches us the correct relationship with our Mother Earth. It is a great responsibility for us to continue our sacred ceremonies so they may heal the bad times that will come for all future peoples.

The Rainbow Tribes that can see the new vision will learn to see, as our tribe does, that the Earth is our Mother. They will try to live a life of balance that nurtures and respects the Earth as they would honor their own mother who gave them birth. It will be difficult for the Rainbow Tribes to find this path of balance because their culture will have taught them that the Earth is only a resource to use for personal gain.

As the Rainbow People seeking balance look for a path, they will explore the way of the ancient tribes of Turtle Island. In my vision I saw a sundance ceremony with the New People of different colors dancing side by side with the future children of our tribe. Also, some of the Rainbow People were pipe carriers in the tradition that White Buffalo Woman has taught to us.

This vision will birth a new beginning, a time of peace and prosperity for all the Rainbow People and the People of our own tribes. We will all join together in the new vision and we will know when the time is near for the white buffalo calf to be born."

Chapter 13

Journey's End

At the time of the longest night Owl called the Council Wheel together. The council fire caused Owl's white hair to glow like a bright aura around his lined face. He signed with his hands while telling his life story, from the time of his birth to the winter night in which they sat. His tale unfolded the rich history of the People of the North Star Valley. He then continued his story into the present moment.

"Like my Grandmother before me, I am called by the Powers to cross over into the Spirit World in the time of winter. I have given my story to this council before I leave so it may be retold and my

*memory will not disappear from the knowledge of
the People. Many of these stories have been told
before; on the other hand no one has heard the
whole story. Many of the stories of White Buffalo
Woman need to be put into our songs so they will
be remembered. If my vision is correct, the survival
of our people may depend on remembering the ceremonies of these stories.*

*Before I leave I will pass White Buffalo
Woman's Pipe to a new keeper. The council member I have chosen is my mate and lifetime friend,
Moonflower. For many winters she has sat in the
south of our wheel and her wisdom has grown with
the turning of the seasons. I also feel that she
would make a powerful Sundance chief if this
council agrees with me.*

*Moonflower, when Eyes of Wisdom passed the
pipe to me I felt that I was not ready to step into
her moccasins. I felt that I was not wise enough to
lead the ceremonies and to do the doctoring for our
people. I then looked around at the other members
of our council and realized I was as qualified as
they were to take Grandmother's place. What I
have found over the years since then is this: The
power comes when we accept the responsibility
given to us by our elders. Over the years I have
grown to love the responsibility of leading the ceremonies that bring the People together. It has also*

been a joy to help people with their healing. You in
turn will grow into the place of power that being
the keeper of our Sacred Pipe will bring."

Night Eagle handed White Buffalo Woman's Pipe to Moonflower. He then embraced her and went around and hugged all the weeping members of the Council Wheel.

As Owl embraced each council member, he tried to impart words of wisdom that would help guide them on their paths. He also realized that only he, Moonflower, and Longtail remained from the original council created by White Buffalo Woman. Although Longtail's eyes were bright and his body thin and muscular, he was very old. It would not be long until Longtail also took his journey into the World of Spirit.

In Owl's farewell embrace around the council wheel, he came last to Longtail. They held each other's shoulders, gazing into each other's tearing eyes. "Longtail, you have been a father to me after the loss of my own father at birth. Your wisdom has expanded my vision and helped me to see a more whole world. You have created your paintings with the power of Father Sky and Mother Earth to awaken them with life. Our sacred stories were brought to life by you and we could see and touch the spirit world of our imagination. The painted stories have helped me to see that our stories were parts of my inner self. When I found these parts in conflict, the stories have helped me find a path toward peace and balance. I love you dearly."

Night Owl and Moonflower left the council together arm in arm and walked through the freezing winter night to their lodge. Moonflower removed her clothes and then helped Owl out of his leggings. She went to where she kept her personal belongings and brought out a small bundle. It was made from sheets of rawhide tied together; she sat the bundle between them next to the fire. Looking into his old wrinkled eyes she spoke:

"Little Owl, when I was a young girl I was very attracted to Stalker and the other young hunters of the tribe. You seemed too quiet and I thought you were not strong. In the end it was your gentle kindness that joined my heart to yours. Choosing you for my mate was the most important and perfect action I have ever taken in my life. Being with you has taught me that the greatest strength is the strength of Spirit.

I knew it was possible that you might leave this Earth before me. Know that I will carry White Buffalo Woman's Pipe with honor; I will also carry on her teachings.

Although this lodge will be lonely and empty without you to share it with, I will live my remaining winters fully and with joy. Until the end of my life you will always be in my heart."

Owl took her hands and replied, "Flower Person, we will be joined together again when you cross over to the Spirit World. And know that although my body will be gone, the love that we shared will live on until we reunite. I feel that our love is everlasting, for it was born in the World of Spirit."

Moonflower carefully unwrapped the sheets of rawhide and inside were many dried flowers pressed between the sheets.

"These are the flowers you brought to me from the mountain top those many winters ago. I have preserved them as a pledge of your love."

She then wove a wreath with the dried flowers for Owl and one for herself, and they placed them on each other's heads. They threaded the remaining flowers into one another's hair, as they had often done when they played together in the meadow.

Within the wrinkled woman with the long white hair Owl could still see the radiant glow of the raven-haired beauty he had fallen in love with. The old couple embraced and made love medicine together covered with the give-away flowers of their youth.

Owl felt the sacredness of the Spirit World enter into the lodge and surround them. The medicine of the Sweat Lodge and Sundance was all around them. Often, Owl had touched the World of the Sacred when making love medicine with Moonflower. This time as they joined together he felt that they were merging with the Creatress and Creator and becoming one with the All That Is.

They lay in an embrace as they slowly returned to the World of Earth. Owl knew his time had come and and he smiled a farewell to Moonflower as he rose. Then, like his Grandmother before him, he left the lodge into the winter night and was never seen again.

Owl walked through the sub-freezing night as the ice crystals were being stirred by the wind in the clear sky. The full Moon reflected on each crystal and it seemed there were little stars dancing in the air. As Owl approached the Medicine Tree, there was a faint rainbow arched over it. The Moon cast a bow with the magic of the frozen particles in the sky. Owl sang the medicine song that Eyes of Wisdom had given to him. He thought about his life and felt that it was finished in beauty. In front of the Sacred Tree there stood a buffalo covered with frost. The buffalo looked white and it reminded him of his first vision dream. With a smile on his face, Owl started running toward the tree, singing his Sundance song. He ran with his arms outstretched and the buffalo charged straight toward him. If anyone were watching they would have seen the frost-covered buffalo charge into Owl's out-stretched arms, killing him instantly.

If we were seeing through Night Eagle's eyes, we would have seen White Buffalo Woman run-ning toward him. As he ran he felt younger and younger, until he was the youth who had first seen White Buffalo Woman. She was shining, and her arms reached out to Owl and they joined together in an embrace.

HO

Epilogue

During the last decade, several white buffalo calves have been born. To many Native Americans and other medicine people, this is a sign of great hope. It is a sign that the healing of Mother Earth has begun, bringing the unification of the black, red, white, and yellow races.

As the age of Pisces is ending and the age of Aquarius is soon to begin, we experience the birth of a new age, the time of a new beginning. Ancient myths may help us through this transition. It is time to build more functioning myths into our culture, and the indigenous peoples may give us powerful roots that our vision can grow from. I feel that our new myths must include seeing the Earth as sacred, as our ancient teachers have taught us. Listen to the words of Chief Seattle in answer to President Pierce's offer on behalf of the United States to buy the tribal land of our Northwest Elder's people:

"How can you buy or sell the sky? The land? The idea is strange to us. If we do not own the freshness of the air and the sparkle of the water, how can you buy them? Every part of this Earth is sacred to my people. Every shining pine needle, every sandy shore, every mist in the dark woods, every meadow, every humming insect. All are holy in the memory and experience of my people.

If we sell you our land, remember that the air is precious to us and shares its spirit with all the life it supports. The wind that gave our grandfather his first breath also received his last sigh. The wind also gives our children the spirit of life. So if we sell you our land, you must keep it apart and sacred, a place where man can go to taste the wind that is sweetened by the meadow flowers.

Will you teach your children what we have taught our children? That the Earth is our Mother? What befalls the Earth befalls all the sons of the Earth.

This we know: The Earth does not belong to man, but man belongs to the Earth. All things are connected like the blood that unites us all. Man did not weave the web of life; he is merely a strand in it. Whatever he does to the web, he does to himself.

We are part of the Earth and She is part of us. The perfumed flowers are our sisters; the bear, the deer, the great eagle, these are our brothers. The rivers are our brothers; they carry our canoes and feed our children.

Each ghostly reflection in the clear water of the lakes speaks to events in the memories of my people. The water's murmurs are the utterances of my father's father.

We love this Earth as a newborn loves its mother's heartbeat. So if we sell you our land, love it as we have loved it. Care for it as we have cared for it. Hold in your mind a memory of the land, as it is when you receive it. Preserve the land for all children and love it as God loves us all.

One thing we know: There is only one God. No man be he red or white can be apart. We are brothers after all."

List of Illustrations

Page viii

"White Otter." White is the color given to north on the Medicine Wheel, the place of wisdom and spirit. Otters, who know all streams and rivers, symbolize the keepers of healing throughout our body's circulatory systems. Native American healers place an otter's hide on their patient to absorb the disease. Afterwards, they shake the hide to disperse the bad energy to the winds.

Page 6

"Sky Father." The eagle symbolizes First Spirit, called Sky Father by the Native Americans. Within Native American culture, birds are depicted as spirit, and the bird-human portrayed in this sculpture represents an archetypal image that appears throughout many different cultures. As Sky Father touches the shield of life, his single spirit becomes many spirits.

Page 16

"Sacred Twins." The People of Rainbow Feathers celebrated Tezcatlipoca as the jaguar deity, the smoking mirror, the keeper of the night sky, and the master of astronomy. Quetzalcoatl is the plumed serpent, keeper of the day sky, and the fire-bringer. Together, these two Mayan deities kindled the first fire of creation.

Page 30

"**Earth Mother.**" White Buffalo Woman is the Native American archetype for the Earth Mother, and she is depicted here blessing the world of Sky Father's spirits with the ceremonial pipe. As she prays over the shield of spirit, the animals awaken with physical life. The world is now both spirit and substance animated with the breath of life.

Page 42

"**Buffalo Shield.**" When a herd of buffalo is attacked by predators, the adults form a protective circle around the young calves. When the Native Americans saw this, they called the buffalos the "keepers of the circle." They knew that everything has a place on the medicine wheel of the Universe, and within this one great circle, there are many wheels that help us to understand life.

Page 50

"**Sacred Gift.**" Our first image of the giver of life is our own Mother. Later we learn to see the Earth as the source of all life. This Mother of Creation recognized by all cultures is given many names, and for the Native American people of the high plains she is called White Buffalo Woman.

Page 62

"Wolf Shaman." According to Native American teaching, each animal has a medicine power that it gives to the Earth. Wolves, called the path finders, know all trails and where they lead. When seeking a new direction in life, it is wise to ask the powers of the wolf for aid in finding the proper path.

Page 70

"White Buffalo Woman Shrine." The Native American legend of White Buffalo Woman began one morning when two men crossing the plains of America saw a beautiful woman approach them, clad in white Buckskin. She came holding a pipe in her hands and taught the men to honor everything in the Universe as she put tobacco in the pipe. The pipe was to be an altar and the center of their ceremonies. As the woman walked away, she turned into a white buffalo.

Page 76

"Sky Mother." Sky Mother is the Sacred Void that existed before the manifest universe. She is the Sacred Womb of creation, the darkness out of which light was born. The lightning bolts are the First Spirit

(Sky Father) flashing through the blackness of the Sacred Void.

Page 84

"**Earth Father.**" In the southwest plains of America, the name for Earth Father is Thundering Earth, and he represents the archetypal Horned God found in the mythology of many cultures. The Horned God dances a circle of protection around Earth Mother, the Creatress. Without him to guard her, the Earth Mother would not have a protected place in which to work her magic of birthing.

Page 90

"**Sweet Medicine.**" The Forest Father, called Sweet Medicine by one of the northern Native American tribes, believed that every part of creation has a lesson to teach. Only when our minds become silent can we hear the language spoken by Mother Earth. Each encounter with an animal can become an oracle, giving special meaning to the moment, especially if the meeting occurs in a sacred space like the Sundance or vision quest.

Page 96

"**Warriors of the Rainbow.**" According to the ancient prophecies of the Native Americans, the spirit of their peoples will be born anew into all of the races that have gathered in our land, and each of the different races of rainbow colors will see that we are all one family. The Rainbow People are not called warriors because they are waging wars on other tribes; rather, they are making war on the parts of themselves that are out of balance. In discovering the balance of the self, they will find harmony with all life.

Page 102

"**The Sacred Tree.**" The Sacred Tree, which Buddha sat beneath and Christ hung upon, appears as a symbol of life across the entire world. Trees create the oxygen that we breathe and make possible our life on Earth. The Sundance Tree is the center of Native American ceremonies, and after the tribe takes offerings to the tree, they give prayers of appreciation, healing and abundance to the Tree of Life.

EPILOGUE

Page 110

"**Miracle.**" The white buffalo calf, by Keith Powell.